underneath

mask

sleaze

life

dream

persecution

Powder

poverty

survive

life

slapping

Beneath

street

lipstick

Lier

nothing

fight

Nightlife

street

Alcohol

hope

spit

poor

line

Sirens

heroin

attack

crying

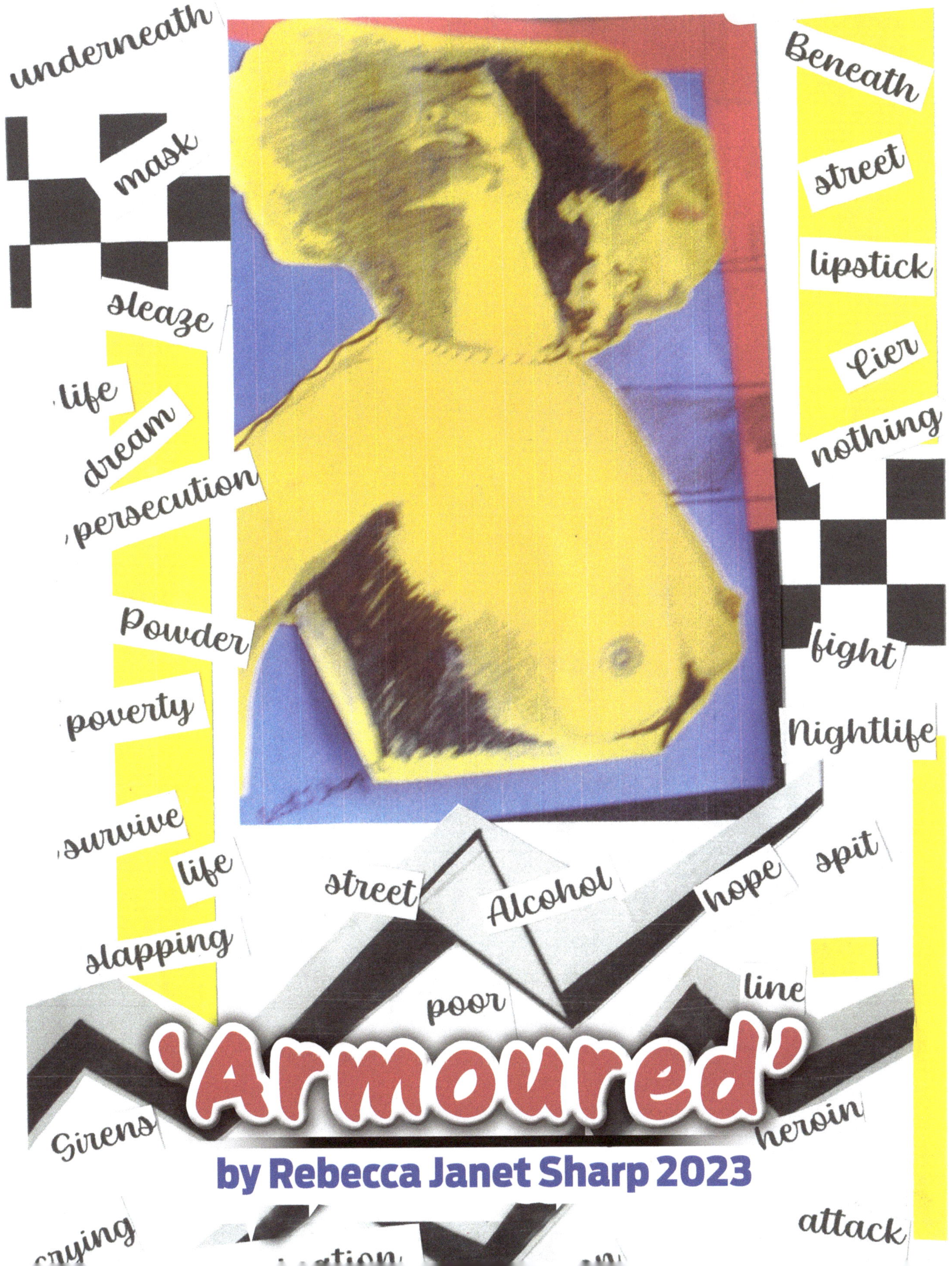

'Armoured'

by Rebecca Janet Sharp 2023

NATIONAL
LIBRARY
OF AUSTRALIA

A catalogue record for this book is available from the National Library of Australia

If any of this content has brought up any concerns, please ring 'Narcotics Anonymous' directly on 1300 652 820 or Life Line on 13 11 14.

All artwork, writing and cover designed by Rebecca Janet Sharp 2023.

Publisher:
ASPG (Australian Self-Publishing Group)
P.O. Box 159, Calwell, ACT Australia 2905
Email: publishaspg@gmail.com
http://www.inspiringpublishers.com

National Library of Australia Cataloguing-in-Publication entry

Author: Rebecca Janet Sharp

Title: 'Armoured'

ISBN 978-1-922920-76-8

To My Dearest Mum
who has always
been there for me,
Thank You.

Brought up amongst chaos, alcoholism, addiction, confusion and loss. One of many, one alone. Left to fantasy and a world of mystery. Kept aside by her Armour.

Childhood took its toll. Teenage years a fortress
for the lonely. As this was a lonely child.
A wild, crazy mixed-up kid. One of aloneness,
rebelliousness, and stripped of any esteem.
Clinging to anyone that could reveal her affection,
kindness and without knowing – love.

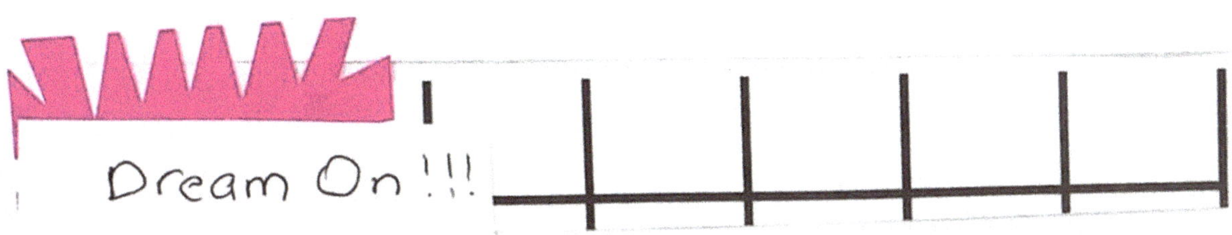

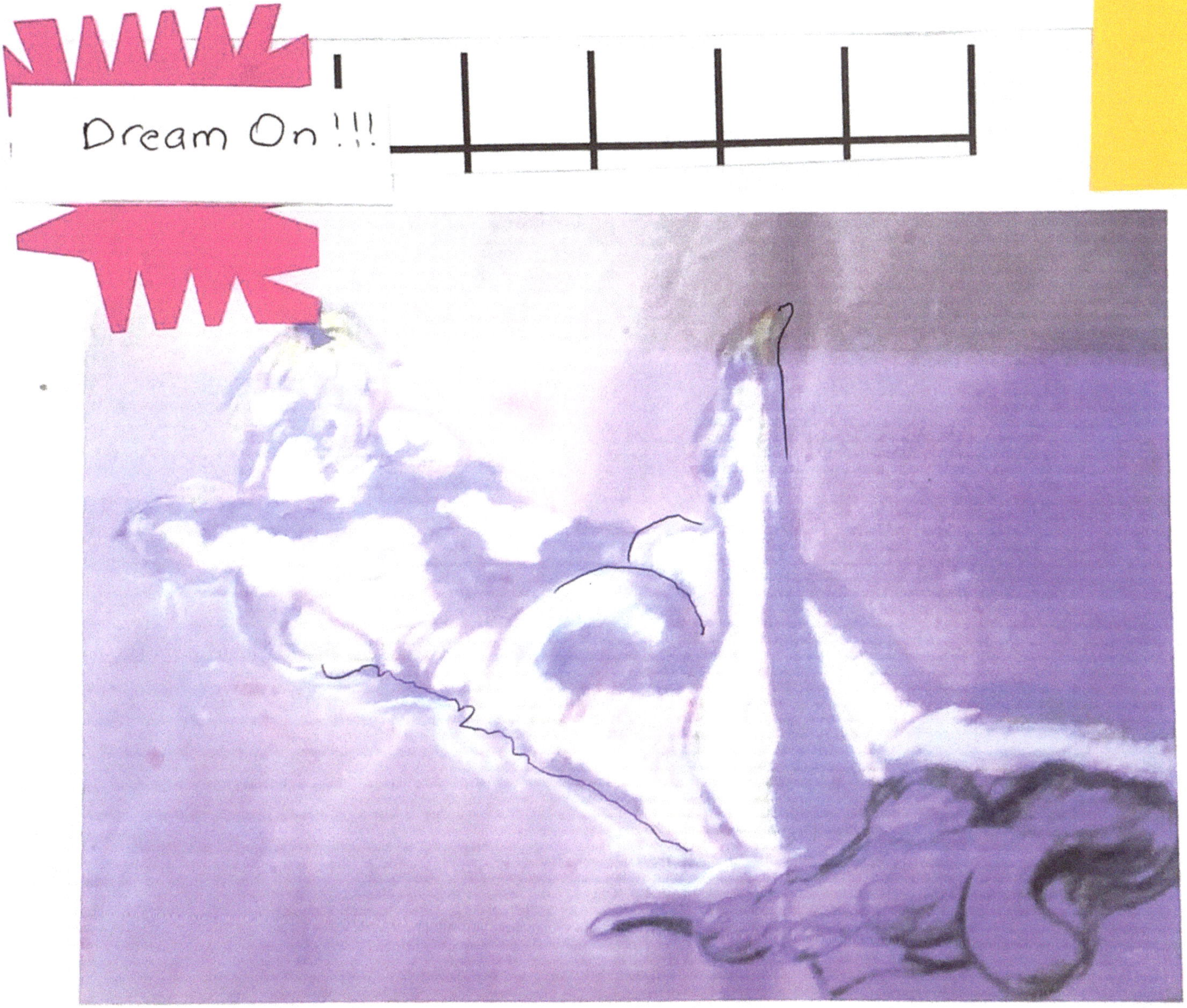

The bottle was her comfort. She learnt. She took to it
like it was liquid gold. An attractive beautiful girl,
yet the hunt was on. On for more, to hide the fear,
the insecurity of an ashamed child, those of
early years of losses and misinformation. Hurt.

She took with her, a brightness, a kindness,
an intelligence that was shunned by the hole that
grew within. Her looks showered by grace and beauty
yet defiant. The world was her oyster but shamed
by a darkness that kept her inner self hidden.

And broken before her time. But, she learnt how to get by.
Her sense of wonderment and imagination.
That was her Armour, her ticket to the world,
with that bottle cradled beside her.

13,14, rape and more fearfulness. She just had no idea.
A way to get through it, but how. Not knowing that
she owned mental illnesses that left her in the darkness.

Shared by many, but not known by herself. Thought!
thought she was just crazy, stupid, horrible she just
learnt to hide amongst the crowd.

Among that time came a child, an unwanted child,
a sexual deliberate act to corner her.
Another whisper of self-hatred and a source of shame.
Though she did love that child. With it more violence,
misunderstanding, and addiction.

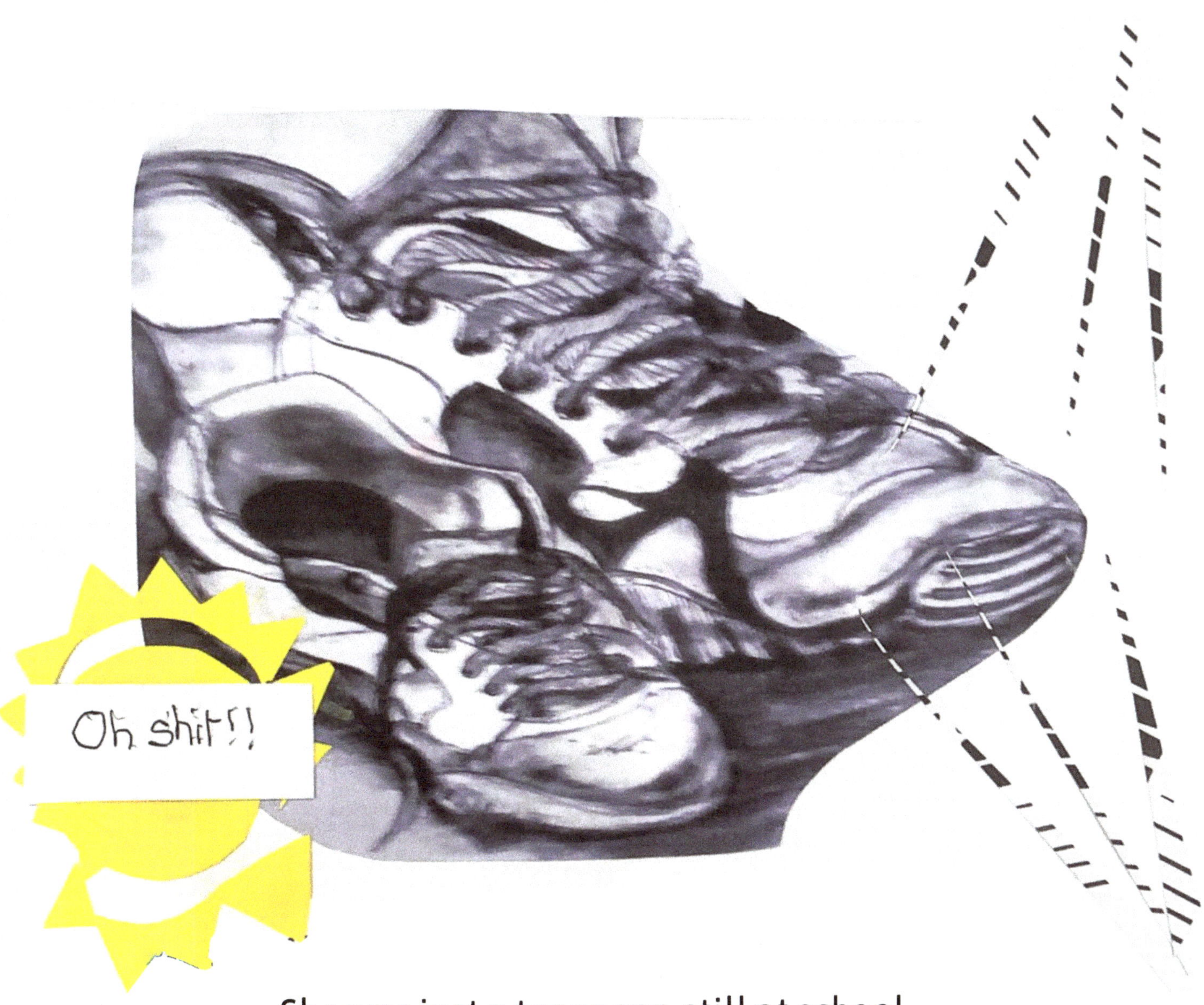

She was just a teenager, still at school.
My goodness so much to bear.

Her own beauty and natural splendidness.
A grace upon her that reflected back to her
in the mirror but not owned by her innermost self.

That took her to many places and faces – there were yet
a few that promised the world yet gave grief and
false securities and hopes of romance.

Art, mystery, glamour, alcoholism. Addiction, chaos, confusion,
postnatal depression, psychotic illness, cigarettes.

And booze, then came the post traumatic stress when down
in town she with an associate was brutally gang raped.
A secret she held so tight as she felt it had been her fault
for hitch-hiking. Which was the done thing. Among thieves.
This was all she knew but how come!!!
Yet this was just a glimpse of the world that she knew.

The world of growing up, learning, achieving,
finding love, marrying – these things were a mystery,
upon mysteries. One she could only view and
compare with, as this girl who saw herself, dirty,
of filth and without – why, why!! Why did she think
that way, it hadn't been her fault, but she saw herself
as a thing, a guttersnipe as we were called
as small children, and she certainly took on that role
and believed the lies she had been told and believed.
Yet there were some stolen possibilities.

It was her armour and her fight that kept her going.
A world of frozen fantasy, she says frozen, because
it was a belief that came stuck in solid ground that –
that one day, amongst all this, the vision would be
revealed to her. That frozen moment would one day
come upon her. Her Armour,
'THE STORY'!!!!

The man in shining armour. THERE WERE the few
that came her way. But alcohol and drugs, music,
took her to yet another plane. The drinking became
more obvious. Sex with strangers, she could still name
them, would dominate her thinking and lifestyle.

Rehabilitations, upon rehabilitations.
The cycle of addiction and getting away.
Hiding. Didn't take them too seriously,
as She as an addict could see that sobriety was yes!
indeed a possibility! Yet was it?

But not for her. 'The big empty', loneliness, a constant associate of kind, was one that dominated her thinking. How could she live without a substance? Yet secretly she didn't want to stop the drinking and dope. She didn't believe she could.

But hoo, here it was – Heroin!!!. Sad to say that she
had actually thought of it as something, that sense
of something that had been missing in her whole life.
She couldn't see her life without it. She really couldn't.
The sense of that extreme sweetness, The feeling
of that high was indescribable. That false sense of
something tasting that good, man!!!!

Are you serious!!!!!!
Heroin to her was the hidden gem.
So manipulating and cruel.

Talking to the devil itself. As it was kill, crush, destroy – her!!!!
Didn't want to know the crap that came with it but survival
was yet another knowing. But she was so broken and messed
up heroin felt grand and if this madness was what she was to
commence, then, so be it. She gave her whole life away for
that elusive high! The same for so many.

Learning street talk was necessary to survive.
And survive she knew well. And she ached for the
instant gratification Heroin gave her that first time.
As it is for every addict. It stole her wholeness that
she didn't know she had. It ripped out her soul and
crushed her to pieces.

She received persecution through family neglect though always maintained a high quality love from her mother and vice-versa. This was obvious through acts that can only be engaged in an

addict's life challenges. She was locked up for theft charges and the obvious charges that come from addiction. Her zest for the taste that enhanced mood and lessen the cravings and humiliation in the loss of control and in the grovelling and painful withdrawal symptoms were becoming worse and harder to bear.

Her means of supporting her habit was – in the beginning –
given to her through sex with her boyfriend. The voices in
her head were getting louder and louder and she really
believed that by substance abuse they were helping but
in the real world it was worsening her condition.

It became necessary to start whoring – prostituting.
Something that sickened her from the inside – out.
Though the need for the taste, that high or as it felt – normality,

as all addicts feel in active addiction. Thieving, prostituting,
grovelling, antisocial behaviour was becoming the norm.
Running from the police became a reality too.

Being held in cells, street hustling began. A very scary place for one really was quite beautifully naïve and good looking, though it happens to many girls she was becoming familiar with. She even witnessed a pregnant prostitute.

Her whole complicated and whole being was being
attacked by others and bad men. Swallowed up
by filth and degradation. Man, the types you come
across along with this lifestyle were indescribable,
yet a necessary thing, with the required drugs and
alcohol needed for the day's hours. Life was hard.

These times were threatening times.
Becoming in the agony of addiction.

Street – hookers, dealers, sleazy greasy men that reeked of manipulation and personal vendetta and gain, drugs, alcohol, events occurring that were life threatening. Like being thrown out of a moving car, guns to the head, diseases, poverty driven monsters coming out of the nights, usually by males wanting sex. Driving around to find an end of the means to rid themselves of lustful thinking and control. Some could see this pathetic means as sad – but deadly at the same time. You just didn't know who was behind the wheel. Only another working girl could understand that anguish.

Suited were the darkness that came of the night.
Darkness that leads the day.

Never knowing if you were going to be ripped off in one or
many other ways. You needed to have your wits about you
suspicion and fear gripped you continuously.

You met with the ugly side of life, of people. Revealing the very worst of mankind. Like war of a kind. As it was to battle she went. Her armour was her thread to humanity.

This girl was a survivor, there was no doubt about that, of mental illness and wit. How did she manage to get through her day. Grapping sleep where it was possible and save to do so. Sex, sex, sex no not sex but filth. No one could understand her self-hatred, and persecuting mind it just went on and on. No end in sight.

Addiction is an ugly misinformed and frightening deadly illness as this was a disease of the mind, only other addicts could understand. Her mother must have been going out of her mind with worry. How could this happen? How could this nightmare stop?

Not only did she not know but Rebecca herself was unable to comprehend. The madness of addiction. It went on and on. The agony, the worship of sorts to drugs and alcohol.

Crazy, frightening moments. Even the police could not stop her.
She would run like the wind to hide from them, but her world was
closing in on her. Some people cared yet none known to her
as she hated her life so much yet that elusive high just too adored.

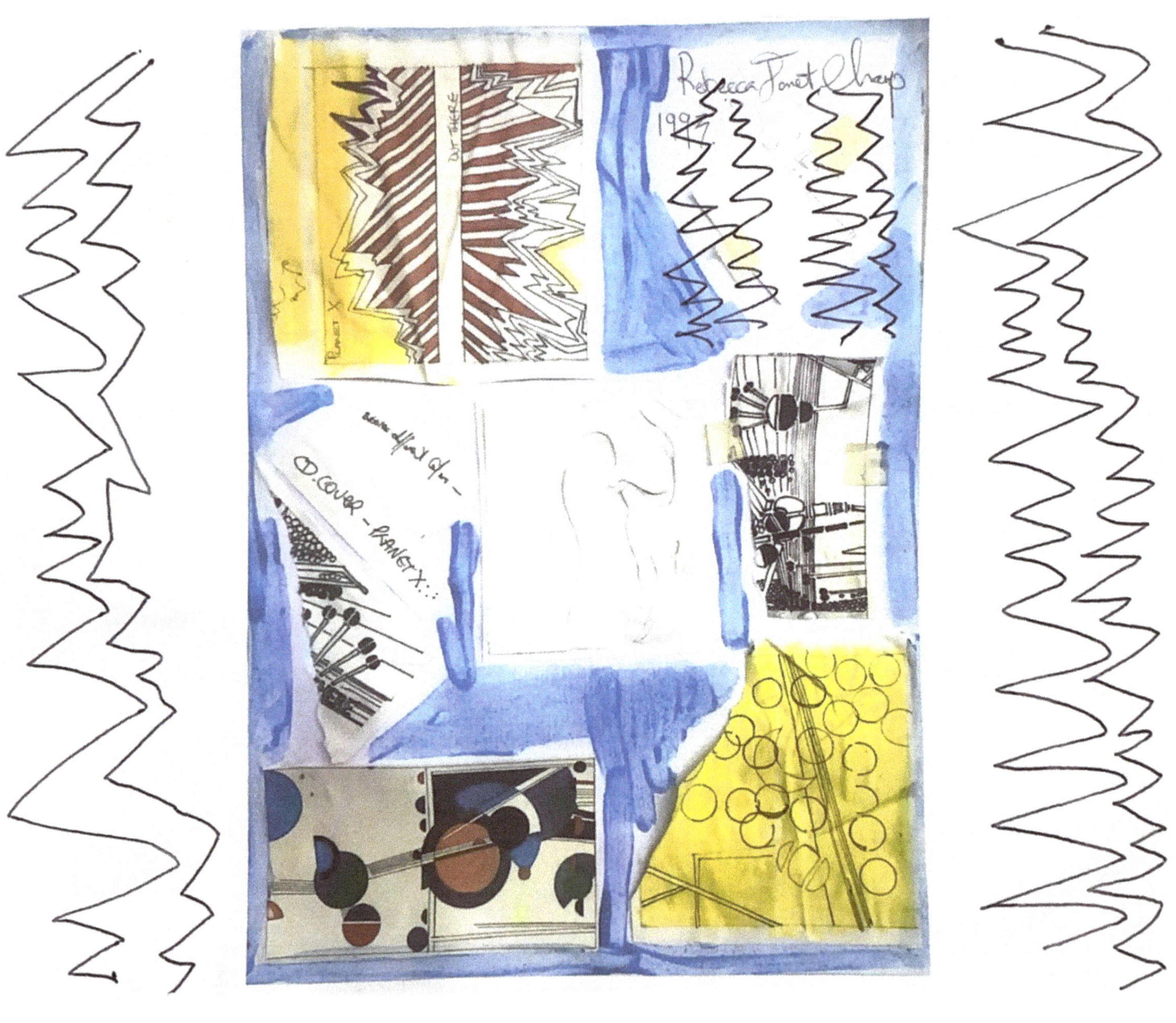

The risk of losing it was too scary and life without
that drug was just too bewildering and fearful.
Not another to ever contemplate.

There were the flights to Sydney, and rehabs
to consider. But for this girl it was unbearable.
Especially since the pain within her physically,
as she really was a bloody mess and needed
attending to. Her belly ached like hell, and why
wouldn't it? - months and months of continuing
using and working the streets was a nightmare in
itself and to contemplate as it was consumed with
fearful events, getting in and out of strangers' cars,
and seriously avoiding the law. But this girl was sick,
really sick, thin and barely alive. Shoes that were
overworn, clothes that were constantly renewed
and at times were stolen.

And make-up well, it had to look good at all times.
As her story, her Armour of that man in shining
armour just might come along. Still madness yet
brave as it was her way of coping with this lifestyle.
As all she cared for was that stone, getting
high, staying at strangers' places
etc. Experience after experience of
sexual advantageous moments as
she without knowing it, still had a
radiance, a look of splendor.

The drugs had taken her to misery, misfortune, constant suspicion of anyone who just looked awful or dangerous, or anybody actually, as it had been her experience of being constantly ripped off even by the other addicts, who were equally looking for ways of grabbing dope for themselves by any means possible. The working girl really is, even today, a victim of much hustling, advantageous moments and difficult experiences by the sleazy men that would be constantly circling the streets to find the one who looked – well – looked like a possible score.

As her days were coming to an end, she couldn't run from
the law anymore. It was impossible for her to run anymore
since her health had declined somewhat so badly, she was
a shadow of her old self. Though the thought of being clean
and sober as she drank bottles of low-grade whiskey a day
was friggen so, so scary. Kings Cross, she became familiar
with, though she was Melbourne born, Saint Kilda streets
she walked, going back and forth too. Dangerous, as danger
gripped the day and worse at night.

A girl on each corner. Man, it was each to their own.
Dog eat dog. Police constantly Pulling up and throwing this
girl in lock-up. Trying to cease the night's dread.
But it was just a bummer, as withdrawals would creep up,
unbelievably nasty. Same too when your money for
the night is stolen constantly. A battle that was frequent
and remembered as living in hell by any addict.
Every muscle and bone aches like crazy. To a degree where
you would do anything to stop the pain that was withdrawal.
That taste was all she thought of to stop the pain.

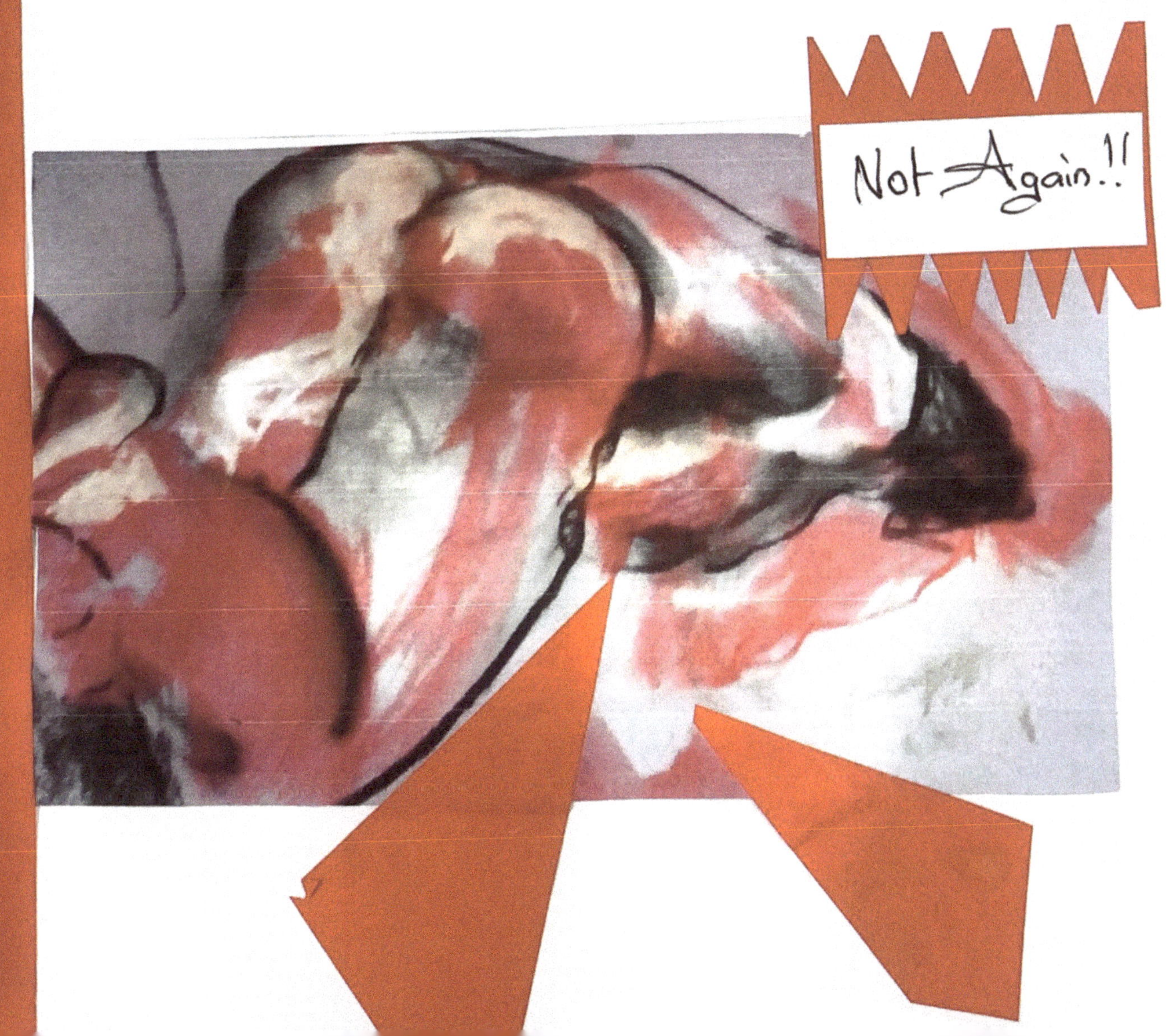

Her Shield, her Armour kept her going, how,
only the universe swayed her way, that kept her going.
Her ability to survive was brilliant and deserving of the
chance of being clean. She was not meant for this life.
There was another coming, and still to her fortune,
was her dear mother that on the occasion would
follow her only to lose track of her since this girl
knew how to slip and slide and become invisible.

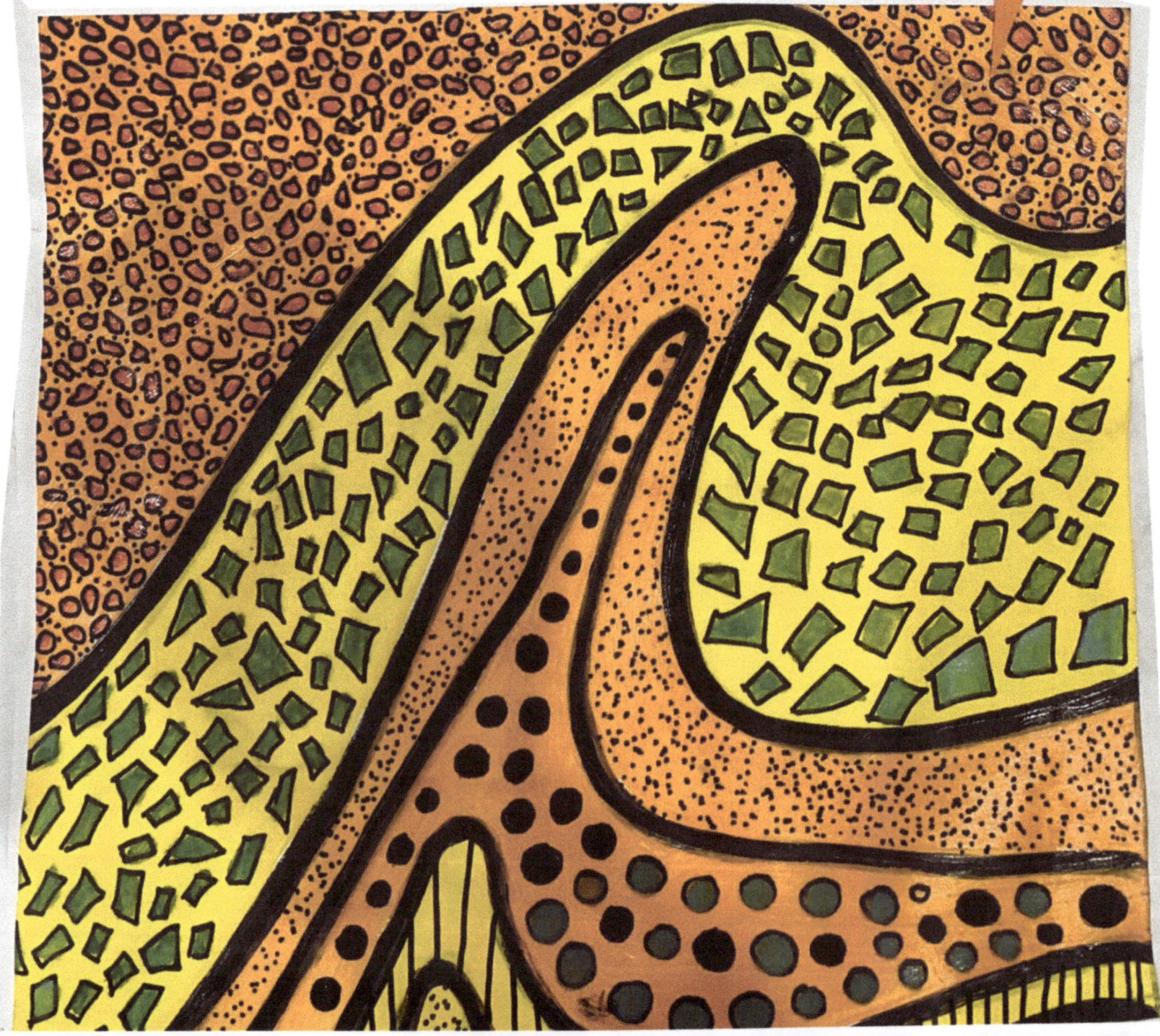

Sometimes behind in a toilet, where she could slip the drugs into her system. Toilets were often sought out as a means of sculling the alcohol down or to get the drugs into her body, not a very convenient way of getting stoned but besides, hygiene was not usually bothered about since getting high was the agenda. Always carrying a bag full of syringes, tissues with blood marks on it, cigarettes, make-up and a bottle of scotch, usually the cheapest bottle and usually going to different bottle shops paranoid of what people behind the bar could be thinking – what if they recognized her?. Ha!!! As if they didn't know.

Her family had shunned her. Even times of verbal
and yes, physical abuse. Times that only taught
her son negative role modelling, so much
so that it ripped that relationship apart.
There was no love, understanding, compassion.

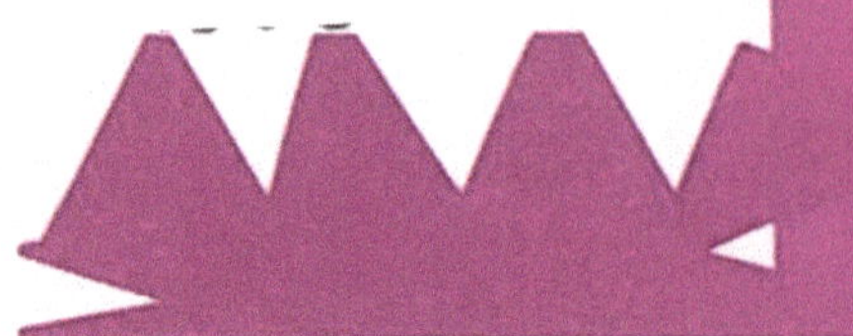

Though her little mum had also been bewildered,
she did stand by her, where no one else dared.
Ashamed and stapled on, the verbal abuse
threatened any means of wanting to get clean,
as this girl, she thought had no one. So, she thought.
The mother thing?

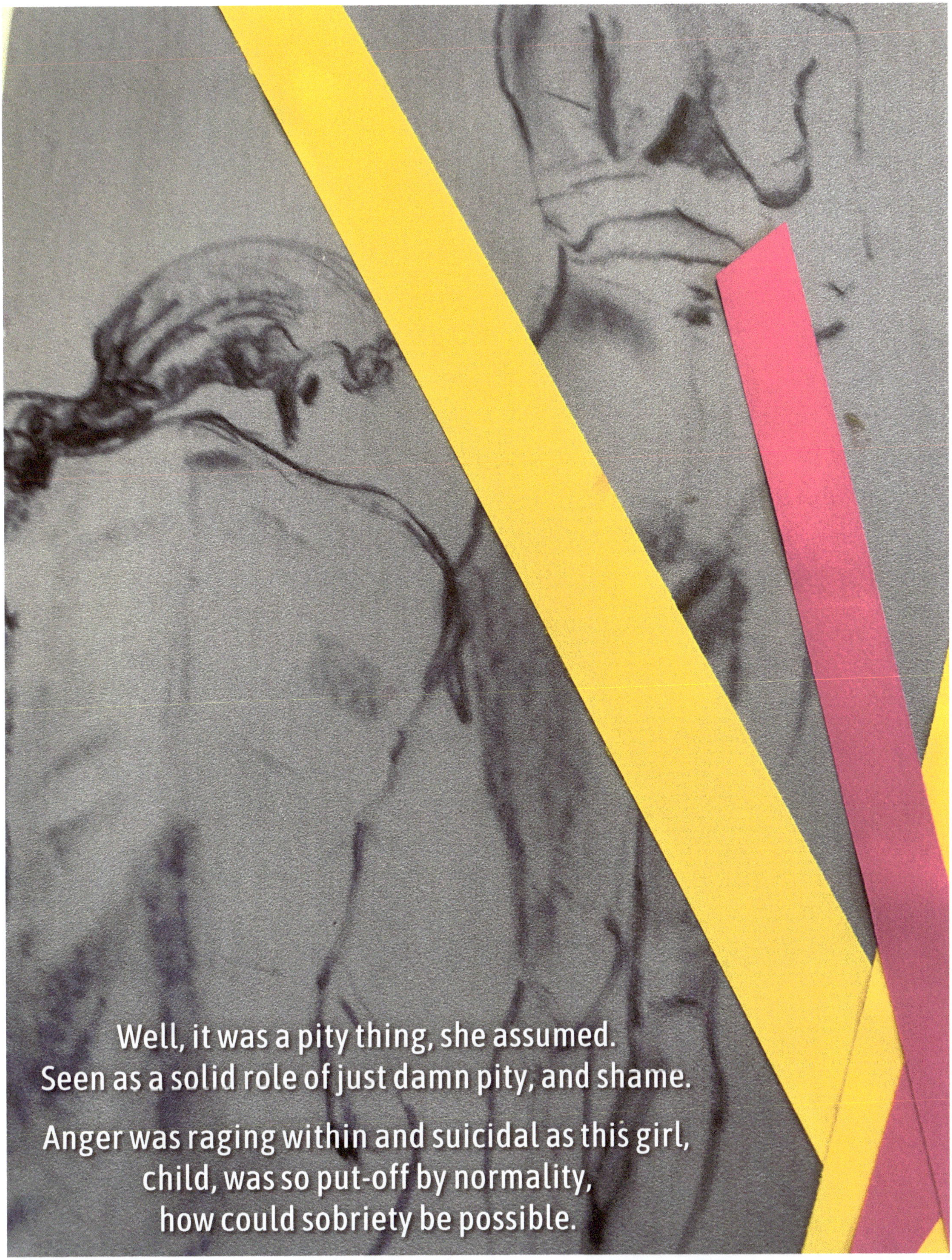

Well, it was a pity thing, she assumed.
Seen as a solid role of just damn pity, and shame.

Anger was raging within and suicidal as this girl,
child, was so put-off by normality,
how could sobriety be possible.

The law had caught up with her, her days as a practicing
user were coming to an end. And so it was she had been
sentenced to rehabilitation with the Salvo's, which she
couldn't and didn't argue with anymore, she was just
too sick to fight. Addiction had its final day. But how
could this girl ever show her face to the world?
Shame and degradation, pity and trauma.
So, traumatized by her experiences of living the
addict life in Melbourne, that living with the Salvation
Army in Sydney was what gave her the escape she
so desperately needed. Her trauma so buried within.
Her heart was broken, her soul destroyed.
Only the Salvo's would take her and that they did.

To Sydney it was, again, this time to Rehab and sick
and tired, so very sore in pain so very unwell to the
point of not even being able to walk by herself.
In fact, she was picked up and carried into rehab.
There to be for 18 months by law. She still was able
to present herself well, strangely enough.

Part of Rebecca was that she, even as a hooker,
dressed in style. Something she carries even to this day.

She reflects often of the first day she was paid for sex,
and she remembers the tears that ran down her face as
how now could her dream – her Armour ever come true now
as she saw herself as being very dirty. Something she was called
as a child by her nasty, sick grandmother, who also would
parade around the house with our underwear on the end of
a broomstick, calling out that we were dirty, dirty children,
dirty creatures. Such feelings would enter her mind a lot and
feelings of shame left her in despair. These feelings came
associated with the lived experience of prostituting,
as now she really, really felt dirty.

These feelings of shame, suicidal, deep, deep depression didn't venture her into the taking of her life as the Armour, the story, the fantasy would often come forth into her consciousness and kept her

going. Though life was unbearable. Somehow, there was a light still within that she had that others could see but not Rebecca. She was devastated, still like being in shock. But she was learning about the disease of addiction. Though worn out, sick and sore, a man approached her with kindness, and she within her mind dreamt of love and romance. Something she really knew nothing about.

In her sick mind this man would just take her to another world. As sick as this was, it was what kept her going. Withdrawals, groups and therapy, she needed to just be left to the care of the Salvo's that after being in the withdrawals area for 2 weeks she went up to the Central Coast, to a farm for women only. Something she really, really needed. Within a couple of months Rebecca found herself in hospital.

She had been ripped apart so badly that surgery was the only option. The doctor, the surgeon, came into her room and said caringly, with a look of worry, said 'I did the best I could'.

Rebecca in a world of her own, mental illness aplenty didn't really understand the seriousness of the surgery as it was still a fog that she lived in. She was told that she wasn't to have sex for two years to allow her body to heal, as he had said that he had to sew her up, the surgery was called 'a division of adhesions'. Rebecca was just floating on the stone that came with being on Pethidine. It's of no wonder the Salvation Army Officer was bewildered by her. She obviously knew that she still had some of

'using drugs' left in her. But one day, this kind man came and gave her a book called 'Narcotics Anonymous'. She read it and broke down in tears thinking someone cared enough about her to write a book about her. This was the first time she had received hope.

Torn apart emotionally, and physically, her spirit was broken, but at that time she fell in love with Sydney. It offered new hope, new beginnings. Never did she want to return to Melbourne. As it had only given to her traumatic experiences. Not to run the town down, but for Rebecca it was a city of nightmares.

Still unaware of mental illnesses, too frightened to find out that she was mad, too horrible or some sort of monster, she happily lived in Sydney, though from one place to another, remained there, renewing her love of painting. Creativity was also a source of being able to express herself as she was learning to be the artist that she is today that encompasses her.

She met some very fascinating and wonderful people. She remained
happily in Sydney for 8 years, doing meetings and where she
earnt an entry into the Sydney School of Art. She did well, earning
a high score for drawing and learnt how much art had played
a very important part and a thread to her heart and soul.

Unfortunately, her mother asked her to return to
Melbourne, The Mornington Peninsula. She had not
dwelled into her past to deal with past traumas,
and found herself eventually returning to using
drugs again. At first, she attended Art School,

where she fortunately continued to be graded with
high scores, and made some beautiful work more
importantly as this girl loved learning.
A skill within itself.

She today still possesses much of her work. How is something else? But the drugs had their way with her again. This time it was the Devil's other drug 'Speed'. She also found herself returning to prostitution. Which she hated even more so. It was years of sacrifice that took her through prostituting, homelessness, so much loneliness and with some lowlife types of people, etc. etc. Yet there were the few that still today, remain friends. It was another dark time that felt like it went on and on. Eventually she became unwell mentally and finally was diagnosed with her mental illnesses. It was through taking marijuana that her illnesses were becoming apparent.

There was some sobrieties. But one day she
just had enough. She no longer wanted to take
drugs and become a sober and clean member of
society. It was a simple decision that she swore
she would never use addictive drugs again.
To this day hasn't. One thing was ridding herself
of toxic people one by one, taking on counselling
and attending meetings. She eventually got
well and continues to understand herself
and talk about her troubles.

Life is sweet and good as she continues to
be creative in making her art come alive.

She also lives with her beautiful girl cat called 'Celecus',
and feels very grateful that she had ceased the drug scene before
Ice had become so prevalent in today's society. Yes, life is good,
she has come alive again. Her dear mum still with her Dementia
still remains her number one fan. Life is what you make it.

Self portrait by Rebecca Janet Sharp 2023

The End